NOBODY'S DOG

(hardcover title: To Catch a Tartar)

NOBODY'S DOG

(hardcover title: To Catch a Tartar)

by
Lynn Hall

Illustrated by
Joseph Cellini

AN
APPLE®
PAPERBACK

SCHOLASTIC INC.
New York Toronto London Auckland Sydney

ISBN 0-590-33893-5

12 11 10 9 8 7   5 6/9

Homeless Pup

No one ever learned where the pup had come from, nor how he happened to be standing in the middle of the dirt track that led from the Yettcairn moors to the farmers' cottages south of the village.

It was Andrew Stewart's border collie, Mirk, that found the pup. Mirk and Andrew had been driving the Stewart sheep home from the moors where the flock grazed during the day. Mirk's attention seldom left the sheep even for a moment, but she smelled the pup in the road, then saw him and quickly turned the sheep aside so that the pup would not be trampled. Head lowered in curious concern, she circled back to the pup and examined him.

Andrew came and stood beside Mirk, staring down at the pup. Andrew was a young man, square-faced and serious.

"What is it you found, girl?"

He bent lower over the pup, which crouched down away from him.

The pup was the size of a small cat, with bony hips, a potbelly, and a head that was too big for the rest of him. His coat was rough and dull, a mixture of black and white hairs, and a few tan ones, so that the resulting color was a rusty streaked gray.

"You're a poor-looking specimen, aren't you?" Andrew said. "And what are you doing out here on the moor?"

Andrew's big hand scooped up the puppy, but then held him dangling in the air while Andrew tried to think what to do about the little nuisance. He didn't want to be bothered by the pup, but his farmer's instinct wouldn't let him walk away and leave any helpless animal to die. And Andrew knew this pup was too young to take care of itself.

Finally, shrugging and motioning Mirk back to her sheep, Andrew tucked the scrap of dog against his ribs and trudged on toward home.

The Stewart croft was very small and very poor, as were all the other farms in the valley. It was only four rocky acres, with an ancient stone shed for the sheep and an equally old white-washed cottage. The cottage was low, with a chimney at either end and two rooms and a loft inside.

It had seemed pleasant enough and roomy enough for Andrew, his wife Morag, and their four-year-old daughter Megan, until last year when Morag's mother had come to live with them. Since that time, it seemed to Andrew that the cottage was hardly big enough to hold him. Morag's mother was everywhere, watching him suspiciously and commenting on everything he did.

When he stomped into the kitchen and set down the pup, the old woman was the first to see the dog and to criticize Andrew for bringing it home.

"Ugly beast, and no good to anybody," she declared. "Andra, ye never had nothin' between your ears but air. Why did ye not leave the beast where it was?"

While the voices quarreled above his head, the pup crouched as low as he could on the smooth stones of the kitchen floor. The past several hours had held one terror after another, and now his mind and nerves could take no more. His world had been snatched and bumped away from him. The first frights still echoed through him — being stuffed into a smelly sack and banged for a long dark time against the side of a huge moving animal; the stunning thud when he hit the ground; the ache in his ribs; the hunger; and now this harsh place.

Suddenly someone else was beside him, a large quiet, slow-moving young woman who capped his head with a gentle hand and set before him a bowl of warm oatmeal. The fear that had filled his head seemed to go out through the woman's touch. The pup leaned into her for a few moments until his trembling was done. Then he moved forward a shaky step and thrust his muzzle into the food.

A Tartar

During the weeks that followed, the pup grew at a
rate that surprised everyone and caused Grandmother to say more than once, "Ye should have
left the beast where ye found him, Andra."

The fact was that Andrew had not intended to
keep the pup. Mirk more than earned her place in
the family by caring for the sheep from which
Andrew earned their living. But the pup was obviously not a sheep dog and was therefore worth-

less to Andrew. To make matters worse, he ate an incredible amount of food. But Andrew was stubborn, and he knew that if he got rid of the pup, it would seem that he was letting Grandmother make his decisions for him. So the pup stayed.

Megan was allowed to name the pup. "Tip," she declared, pointing to the white tip on his tail. And so he was named, but even from the first the name failed to stick to him. Megan called him "Puppy," Morag usually referred to him as "the poor wee tyke," Grandmother simply called him "the beast," and Andrew tried not to notice the dog at all.

It became harder and harder not to notice him. By the time he was four months old, his back was as high as Megan's waist, and he was still growing so fast his bones almost creaked with the stretching. Often his joints ached from the pull of tendons and muscles.

His fear of the cottage and the people in it lasted no longer than the first night. After that he galloped and snuffled over every inch of the cottage and the garden outside. He understood that this was his place in the world and that these were his people.

His special love was Megan, who was lower

than the others. Her face was often just inches away from his own. She was the only one who had time to spend with him, and she shared his curiosity about what was under stones and behind furniture.

They ran side by side over the rocky ground, stumbling, tumbling, rolling to a stop with their faces close to the miniature jungle of grass blades and heather roots, where creatures so tiny you could hardly see them lived in a world of their own.

At first, when they ran, Megan slowed her steps to match the pup's. But as the summer months passed, it was the young dog who had to slow his galloping strides so that he didn't leave Megan behind.

By autumn his legs were much longer than Mirk's, and he stood as tall as the largest sheep in the Stewart flock. His tail was a bony, straggle-haired whip, as strong as a scythe. His head had grown long and lean, but it lacked the beauty of the collie's head. His bottom jaw jutted forward crookedly, and his lower teeth showed between his lips.

To Megan it was a clown's smile, but not to the others. Morag said, "Poor tyke, he'll have trouble

eating, later on, with that crooked jaw." Grandmother said, "Ugly beast," and Andrew said, silently, "Worst undershot jaw I ever saw. Poor breeding behind him, if he's got any breeding at all."

Sometimes a shadowed memory came back to the dog, a memory of terror and abandonment. It brought a wash of fear, but the fear was followed by a mixture of relief and joy. He felt the security of home and family around him, and the joy rose wildly inside him. When this feeling came on him, he was driven to race in frantic circles in and out of the cottage, around the yard, through the kitchen door, up onto Andrew's chair, and off again until someone caught him and held him.

"He's daft," Grandmother would mutter.

On one such whirlwind of joy he crashed into the kitchen table just after Morag had set supper on it. Dishes flew and broke on the stones of the floor, and oatmeal and mutton stew splashed everywhere.

When the dog had been shoved outdoors, the mess cleaned up, and the shouting between Andrew and Grandmother over with, Morag said flatly, "That's all there'll be of having the dog in the house. I'll not have my home made a wreck of, and good food wasted. Crying won't change my mind, Megan, so hush."

Later, over a silent supper of parsnips and cold potatoes, Grandmother said, "Ye ought to get rid of the <u>beast</u>, Andra, like I've been telling ye all along. Ye haven't got the sense to know when ye've caught a tartar."

Megan was following the conversation closely, fearful that her dog might have to go. "What does that mean, 'caught a tartar'?" she asked quickly.

Her grandmother frowned down at her from across the table. "It means ye've taken on more than ye can handle. Ye've got more of a foe than ye thought ye had when ye started the battle. That's what it means, and if your father had anything between his ears but air — "

"Mother," Morag said quietly, and Grandmother went back to her potato.

After that the pup was seldom called Tip. The name Tartar suited him so much better that even Megan found herself using it.

The Accident

It was a sunless afternoon in November, and The Tartar lay stretched out on the stone sill of the cottage, with his back to the kitchen door. He wanted very much to be inside the cottage with Morag and Megan, but since that was forbidden he liked to lie where he could hear their voices.

He had just come back from the moor, where he had followed Andrew and Mirk when they took the sheep out to graze. For some time he had been aware of the love between Andrew and Mirk, of the way Andrew's hand dropped to stroke Mirk's head and the way the collie flattened her ears in pleasure under his touch. The Tartar felt a puzzled kind of longing shiver through his great body when he watched them.

Today he had gone with them, following Mirk as closely as he could while she moved deftly behind and around the sheep. It seemed to The Tartar that there was some connection between the things Mirk did with the sheep and the love that he sensed between her and Andrew. With great clumsy bounds the young dog tried to do what Mirk was doing. He galloped around the sheep, and in his joy he began barking wildly. The sheep scattered and he gave chase, delighted at the way the game was going.

But his efforts brought no stroking hand on his head, no soft-voiced praise from Andrew. To his amazement The Tartar found himself angrily ordered home, and the orders were punctuated by stones and clods of dirt hurled at him by his furious master.

Now he lay on the sill stone with his spine pressed hard against the kitchen door. His mind was confused, and something deep inside him was hurt. It was a deeper bruise than the one on his hip, from one of Andrew's rocks. He had tried to earn Andrew's love, and he didn't understand what he had done wrong.

Cold winter blew across the moors from the distant sea, and parted The Tartar's coat. He got up, scratched, and turned on the sill stone, then settled back down in a curled position. He sighed, and strained to hear the voices inside.

Suddenly the door behind him opened, and Megan came out with Andrew's lunch basket under her arm.

"Wear your rokelay," Grandmother bellowed from inside the cottage. Megan ducked back inside and snatched her blue cape from its hook.

Grandmother's voice went on. "Child has no more sense in her head than her fa — " Megan shut the door and leaped down the step, flinging one arm around The Tartar's neck for a quick hug as the two of them jostled down the path and into the lane.

With Megan beside him, the shadows left The Tartar's spirit. He leaped in huge circles about the little girl; he snatched a twig from the lane and raced away with it, then turned and hurtled back past Megan, daring her to take the stick away from him. In his joy he clamped down on the stick, and it broke in his mouth. He skidded to a halt and looked foolishly at Megan, who laughed at him. It was a lovely sound to the dog's ears, and it brought to life the wild happiness that lay within him.

He made a low rumbling noise deep in his throat. It sounded like a growl, but it was merely his way of letting out the joy that grew too strong to be contained. Again Megan laughed.

Encouraged by his audience, The Tartar looked around, saw another stick, and attacked it in a furious mock battle. He looked up to see if Megan was watching, but she had passed him and was near the top of the hill, where the lane entered the Yettcairn moors. Grabbing his stick, The Tartar raced after her, intending to circle her and get her attention.

But he was running too fast, and his long awkward legs were out of control. He swerved to miss her, but his hip struck her. She cried out as she fell.

The Tartar turned back to where the child lay. He put his muzzle in her neck, nudged, snuffled, licked. But she did not move.

He whined softly; he pawed at her cloak.

Suddenly Andrew was there, bending low over Megan.

"Get away, you great brute. Look what you've done to my baby. Get out of my sight!"

Abandoned

Several hours later Dr. McTay came out of the bedroom and walked heavily across the kitchen to the waiting Stewarts.

"She's awake now," he said. "I think she'll be all right, but it was a nasty blow. There may be trouble later. We'll just have to wait and see. You say she fell down?"

"That brute of a dog knocked her down," Andrew said. "He ran crashing into her, and she hit her head on a rock. I should have got rid of him. I should have left him on the moor when he was a wee pup."

For once Grandmother said nothing. Morag poured the doctor a cup of tea and set it silently before him.

The four talked in subdued voices until the doctor's cup was empty.

"I'll be on my way," Dr. McTay said, rising and handing his cup to Morag. "Thank you for the tea, Morag; you brew a stout cup."

"No need to rush off, is there?" Morag asked.

"I'm afraid so. I have to make a stop down by Dumfries, and that's a long drive on a night like this."

Andrew raised his head suddenly. "Dumfries, you say. Would you be going anywhere near my cousin Jock's place?"

"Right by the door."

Without looking in Morag's direction, Andrew stood up. "I'd like to ride over with you, then. I'll be taking the dog. Jock will keep him, and the brute will be out of sight before Megan is up and about. It's for the best," he added, looking hard at Morag as she started to protest.

The Tartar had been lying outside the door listening to the voices. He was disturbed. Something was wrong inside the cottage, something that somehow had to do with him. Ever since he had followed Andrew home and watched the man carry Megan inside the house, The Tartar had remained pressed against the kitchen door. The few times that Andrew or Morag had opened the door, they had stepped wordlessly over or around him.

Now the door opened again, and Andrew and the strange man came out. The Tartar rose and cautiously wagged his tail, unsure of Andrew's feelings toward him. Suddenly he felt a circle of rope around his neck. Andrew's rough hands tied the knot, then pulled until The Tartar found himself going with the men toward the old car that stood in the lane.

The ride was at first frightening, then exciting to The Tartar. He had never been near a car before; the Stewarts were much too poor to have one. As soon as he was used to the smell and the noise and the motion, he began enjoying his position. He nearly filled the small back seat of the car, and his head hung over Andrew's shoulder. The night wind blew into his eyes and ears and mouth. The world rolled past at a wonderful speed. He loved it.

After more than an hour of riding, the car stopped, and Andrew hauled The Tartar out.

"I'll pick you up on my way back," Dr. McTay called out, and Andrew waved in answer.

A house, somewhat larger than the Stewarts' cottage, stood beside the road, its window light shining out at Andrew and The Tartar.

"Come along now," Andrew muttered. "Jock will give you a home, and he has no wee children you can hurt with your rough ways. I know you didn't mean the lass any harm," he ended on a softer tone, "but if we kept you, it might happen again, and worse."

Andrew's knock was answered by a little man who seemed to be all whiskers and wheeze. He looked rather startled at the sight of The Tartar, but invited Andrew and the dog to sit by his fire nevertheless.

Andrew explained what had happened to Megan, and why he must get rid of The Tartar. "So I thought of you, Jock, living here all alone without a dog to guard you and keep you company, and I thought you might be willing to take the animal. I don't know what else to do with him."

Jock stared down at The Tartar. "Och now, Andra, it's a rare big beast. And ugly. I don't believe I've ever put eyes to such a dog as that.

No, I'd have no use for him, nor any liking, either. He fair puts the frights in me, just looking at them teeth of his."

Andrew waited silently, hoping. The Tartar looked from one to the other of them, hesitantly moving his tail against the floor. They were talking about him. He strained to understand.

"No, Andra." Jock shook his head. "The beast would cost more to feed than I do meself. A waste of money. I'd like to help you out, but you know how I feel about wasting my money."

Andrew rose, said his good-byes, and drew The Tartar out of the house behind him. For a long time the man stood, undecided, then he strode off across the open fields behind his cousin's house, walking faster and faster. The Tartar trotted happily beside him, his huge head carried high into the salt-smelling wind.

At length they stopped beside a small birch tree.

"This'll do," Andrew muttered. "You'll be able to chew through the rope without any trouble, and you'll find youself a new home. Just don't try to follow me. I'll not have you back."

He walked away, but when The Tartar moved to follow, the birch tree yanked him back by the neck and held him. For a few moments he thrashed against the rope. Then, whining softly, he sat and watched Andrew disappear into the darkness.

Free but Lonely

For a long time after Andrew had gone, The Tartar sat staring through the night, aching to hear the first sound of returning footsteps. The huge young dog trembled with the wrongness of being here, in this strange meadow, attached to no human being. Dim shadows of the earlier abandonment came up from the bottom of his memory, and, in his mind, he was a tiny pup again, crouching terrified in the middle of a moor lane.

The wind made him uneasy. It smelled of fish

and salt water, unfamiliar smells that should not be there. The sounds that came to him were wrong, too. They weren't the sounds of the Yett-cairn moors. He had a sense of being off-center, somehow, of being far to the left of where he belonged.

It was the rope that held him in this wrong place. He turned and began chewing at the stout rope, working it farther and farther back in his crooked jaws to where the powerful new teeth had just come through. At last, when his jaws ached with the effort, the strands of the rope began to part. The Tartar lunged, throwing all of his weight into the rope. It broke.

He set off at a gallop after Andrew. Freedom and motion began to lift his spirits. Once or twice he barked, sending a message to Andrew that he was coming.

He ran through the black meadow searching for Andrew, for the house where they had sat together, for the car or the road home. Suddenly a road appeared, crossing his path. He stopped, trotted back and forth with his nose to the road and his tail lashing.

He found no trace of a familiar scent, but after a few moments of hesitation he turned and began to follow the road in the direction that led away from the sea smells.

All night he trotted, and by morning the sea smells were gone from the air. But they were not replaced by any of the more familiar smells of sheep and peat fires, smells that would tell him he was going in the right direction. Not knowing what else to do, he continued following the road he was on. His legs were tired by now, and he was hungry. In the excitement and worry over Megan's accident last night, no one had remembered to feed the dog.

As the sun cleared the rim of the distant mountains, the road took him through a small village. The Tartar slowed to a walk, lifted his head, and pulled into his nostrils the welcome scent of people. People meant food, care, a hand on his head, or a small arm around his neck. His tail began to move from side to side in anticipation.

The village appeared empty except for one small roadside cottage. A short stout woman was bending down, on her doorstep, to set a bowl of bread and milk before the cat who stood at her feet. Food and company, together. The Tartar's head lifted, and his heart.

Veering from his course, he leaped the low garden fence and approached them. The cat arched his back and spat furiously; the woman flapped her apron and shouted, "Go 'way with ye, ye great ugly beast. Ye're trampling on me bluebells, and ye're frightening the poor wee kit."

The cat stood in battle pose beneath his mistress' skirts and hissed his taunts at The Tartar.

With a woeful look at the woman and the bowl of food, The Tartar turned and left the garden, accidentally breaking flower stalks as he went.

A few miles away, in a larger town, he had better luck. He saw a small terrier lying curled in the sun on a cottage sill stone, and beside the dog was an uneaten dish of oatmeal and egg scraps. The dog was very old and very fat, and she greeted The Tartar's approach with a slow but friendly wag of her tail. The two touched noses; then, cautiously, The Tartar moved his head toward the food. The terrier ignored him. In three gulps the food was gone, and so was the worst of the emptiness-pain in his stomach.

Suddenly he heard footsteps inside the cottage, moving toward the door. The memory of the angry apron-flapping woman awoke a new instinct in the dog, and this instinct sent him dodging out of sight around the corner of the house as the door opened.

The voice of an elderly man said, "Well now, Abby, I'm glad to see your appetite is better. I was getting worried about you, little lass." The door closed again, and when The Tartar peered around the corner, man, dog, and dish had disappeared.

The days passed. The Tartar followed first one road and then another, through villages that began to look alike to the heart-weary dog. None of them was Yettcairn. None of the crofters' cottages scattered through the valleys was the Stewarts'.

At first his whole mind was filled with Andrew and Megan and the intensity of his search for a scent, a feeling, an instinct, that would direct him home. But as one day followed another, he began spending more and more time hunting for enough food to keep him alive. His longing for the security of home, for the touch of those hands, was growing stronger every day, but the instinct to survive was even more insistent. His search for the Yettcairn moors, and the Stewarts, became diluted by the more pressing search for the day's food.

Gradually he adjusted to his new way of life,

but always in the center of him was a feeling of loss, of the lack of a vital part of his life. He remembered the soft sound of the woman's voice, and the high exciting sound of the little girl's. He remembered the way it felt to have a small arm squeezing his neck, a child's body flung against his own in some wild and silly game. He remembered the rare but deeply precious moments when Andrew's hand would rest on his head and smooth back his ears. Sometimes at night, just as he was falling asleep in a haystack or under a roadside hedge, a whimper escaped with his final settling sigh.

Winter got down to serious business, and The Tartar had less luck finding food set out on doorsteps or left in barns. He began catching an occasional rabbit or field mouse, and so he survived, but his pony-sized body constantly craved more. Ribs and hipbones showed through his coat, and hollows appeared above his eyes, making his head even uglier than it had been.

He covered the counties along the England-Scotland border, following a road for a while, then veering off cross-country in answer to homing instincts that grew weaker with each month that passed. When the urge for human companionship grew unbearably strong, he found a village or town and trotted slowly from street to street, always alert for a coaxing hand, an affectionate voice.

Sometimes he found them. Sometimes, for a day or a few days, he was invited to sleep in a woodshed or under a porch, and was given scraps of food. But times were hard, the country was poor, and few people were willing to accept on a permanent basis a stray dog who stood three feet high and ate endlessly. The temporary friends The Tartar found were usually adults, but it was the children for whom he longed, the children, whose love of running and tumbling, exploring, touching with love, matched his own.

His life was tolerable, but the loneliness remained, and slowly grew.

"Get away, dog."

On an afternoon in early summer, The Tartar trotted into a small but busy market town. The streets were filled with flocks of yearling lambs being driven to the sales pens, and with farm people who had walked miles over the fields to shop and visit.

High spirits bubbled through the dog. He trotted, head up, nose sorting through all the smells in the air. The longing for people was strong in him today, and it excited him to be surrounded by voices. Men's low tones, children's shouts, women's laughter, made an orchestra of loved sounds in The Tartar's ears. He had been too long alone. He had not the nature of a stray dog; the deepest part of him needed a master.

A pinprick of irritation behind one ear made him sit suddenly, to dig at the flea with a hind foot. Long after the flea was gone he went on scratching, just for the luxury of it. When he stopped, he noticed a very small boy standing not far away, watching him. The child's mother was looking in the other direction, talking to a friend.

"Horsie," the child said, as he held out a fat hand toward The Tartar.

Delighted at the invitation, The Tartar came smiling and thrashing his tail. He moved his muzzle over the boy's face, which smelled of milk and chocolate.

"Nice horsie."

Small hands reached for The Tartar's nose and left ear.

"*No*, John-boy," came a sharp command from above. "Get away, dog." A foot and a flapping purse shooed The Tartar away.

"Nice horsie," called the wistful small voice.

The Tartar moved away through the crowd. As he neared the sheep pens, a flock of Cheviot ewes filled the narrow street and came baaing down at him. He turned into an even narrower side street.

At the far end were three children, squatting around a ring drawn in the dirt. They were intent on a formation of marbles within the circle.

It was the girl who first noticed The Tartar.

"Come here, dog," she commanded.

The two boys raised their heads. "He's a big one, ain't he," one boy said. "Never saw him around here before."

The girl held out a hand, and The Tartar went to her, his tail thrashing so hard he could barely walk straight.

The boys went back to their game, but the girl began talking to The Tartar. She stood close beside him and rubbed back his ears until his eyes were drawn into long narrow slits. She wiped her nose on the back of her hand and walked once around him. She took his tail in both hands and swung it as though it were a jump rope. She sat on the ground and pulled one of his huge feet into her lap to examine his toenails.

Under her attentions, The Tartar felt the old immense joy beginning to rise within him. He began racing around and around the girl in small hard circles. She laughed at him, and he raced faster.

"You're daft," she shouted.

She picked up a stone and tossed it. The Tartar bounded after it, attacked it, and killed it, and brought it back to her in triumph.

"Good dog. Fetch it again."

The praise was almost more than he could bear. Love surged up inside him, and because he had no way of holding what was dear to him except with his mouth, he closed his great jaws around her arm. His heart was gentle but his jaws were powerful and his head was muddled with excitement.

Suddenly the girl screamed. "Help. Get him off. He's killing me!"

Her scream was a knife that cut through The Tartar's joy. He leaped aside, landed with two feet on the rolling marbles, recovered his balance, and stood trembling, head and tail low.

The girl took her hand away from her arm and looked at the wound. There was no blood, only small dents in the skin from The Tartar's teeth. But the fun was gone. The girl disappeared into one of the doors that lined the streets, and the boys went back to their game.

The Tartar moved away and headed for the open country.

Something in Common

The summer passed. In The Tartar's memory all that was left of the Stewart family was the hunger they had given him for a master to love and serve.

When autumn came, The Tartar noticed something that he had all but forgotten over the summer — the fact that in each village there was one building filled with children, and that the children came pouring out of the building every few hours, to play in the yard.

At first he had bounded in with them, scattering their games of tag and statues. Usually the children took one look at his huge size, his ugly head with the bottom teeth showing, and his whipping tail. Then they got away from him as fast as they could, leaving The Tartar to stand, bewildered, in the center of the yard, his tail wagging slower and slower. Sometimes a larger, braver child approached him, but almost always a teacher came running from the building to chase The Tartar away before a friendship could be started.

It was an October morning, green and gold and rich smelling. The Tartar stood on the brow of a low hill, looking down at the village of Tideside. It was just a string of fishing cottages along a seawall, with Wigtown Bay sparkling in the sun beyond it. At one end of the village, a schoolhouse stood in a small clearing between a forest of oak trees and the seawall.

The Tartar moved toward the school. It was nearly a year, now, that he had been alone, and

today the loneliness was heavy in him. His ears picked up the sound of children's voices, reciting beyond the open windows of the school, and he followed the sound with his heart as much as his ears.

He settled into the underbrush at the edge of the playground, and within a few minutes the doors opened and a dozen children came pouring down the steps and into the sunlight. Each carried a packet of lunch.

They settled into pairs or trios, on the steps, on the crude seesaws, or merely in the grass. Only one remained alone.

He was one of the older boys, a very large boy who looked as though he were going to grow up to be a fat man. He was eating standing up, leaning against a tree trunk near The Tartar and glancing from time to time at two much younger boys sitting near him. When he had eaten his lunch of oatcake and one small green apple, he moved toward the smaller boys.

The Tartar watched him. Something about the boy drew The Tartar's attention, perhaps the solitude of the boy, the feeling of belligerent loneliness that The Tartar sensed.

The boy made a playful grab at the bread and

cheese in the hands of the smallest boy. Voices came to The Tartar, a rough, teasing voice and two small, angry, rather fearful ones. Then the larger boy was walking away, smiling and eating bread and cheese, while the young child ran toward the teacher, sobbing angrily.

The teacher approached. He was a thin bald-headed man who looked as though he might enjoy cracking young knuckles with his stick.

"Duncan," the man called harshly, "come here to me."

The large boy turned away for an instant, to finish chewing the bread and cheese, and in that instant his eyes met The Tartar's. Boy and dog stared at one another for that flick of time; then the boy turned to face his punishment.

"Duncan, you took Geordie's lunch away from him again, did you not?" The teacher's voice was both angry and weary.

Duncan didn't answer, but stared out into the air in front of him. From the edge of the yard, The Tartar watched. He sensed the tension in the air, and he strained to understand what was happening.

The teacher went on. "You've an ugly way about you, Duncan Burn, and I fair suspect you'll have no friends left in the world by the time you're a man. Why are you always doing such hateful things to the wee children, Duncan? Do you enjoy being a bully?"

Duncan's round face grew red, but still he didn't answer.

"You're getting too big for a proper whipping, which is what you need," the man said with a sigh. "So you'll stay after class and split wood for the stove. One hour."

The teacher went to the schoolhouse door and rang a small bell, and all the children began disappearing into the building. The small boy Geordie turned suddenly toward Duncan and, quick as a hummingbird, stuck out his tongue, then ran for the shelter of the building. Duncan made an equally fast face, but before he followed the others inside, he looked again in The Tartar's direction.

"You're uglier than I am, even."

The Tartar struck the ground with his tail and started to rise to go to this boy who had noticed him and spoken to him. But the boy was running in a heavy, awkward way toward the door.

Through the afternoon The Tartar stayed in the woods behind the school, listening to the voices that came through the open windows.

Every now and then he heard Duncan's voice, the voice that had spoken to him. An odd feeling had taken root in the great gray dog, a feeling of rightness that had to do with the big boy. In that instant when the boy looked at him, The Tartar sensed a loneliness in the boy that was very much like his own.

Inside the school, Duncan Burn sat through the long afternoon with his ears closed to what was going on around him. All he could hear was the echo of the words, "You've an ugly way about you...no friends left in the world by the time you're a man...ugly...no friends..."

He was disgusted with himself and with the things he did, but because he could not bear to think of what kind of person he was becoming, he turned his anger toward the teacher instead. And toward Geordie, for tattling.

Still, a part of him was glad he had taken Geordie's lunch. It proved that he had the power to make Geordie afraid of him. It proved that he had the power to make the teacher angry. And if he couldn't have friends, having power was the next best thing. Having the teacher mad at him was better than being ignored, or being teased for being big and clumsy.

Besides, the bread and cheese had helped a little in easing the hunger he always felt. Duncan's family was the largest and poorest in a village of large, poor families, and this year the fishing had been worse than usual for Duncan's father.

There was never enough food to go around, and there was never enough attention to go around, either. Duncan remembered being a very small boy, like Geordie, fussed over by his mother and poked and tossed by his father. He had long ago become too big and too old for fussing and tossing, but the need was still there. He often daydreamed about how good it would be if his parents would only take the time to notice him now, just look at him and listen to him without giving most of their attention to the other children.

Long ago Duncan had learned that there was one sure way to get the attention of his parents and teacher. Be bad. Cause trouble and someone would come running. Pick on Geordie or one of his own small brothers. It worked every time. The more he did it, the less he liked himself, but he needed the attention it brought him, and he couldn't seem to stop.

An hour of splitting wood after school. It wouldn't be too bad, he thought. He was strong and he liked splitting wood, showing off in front of the other children, swinging the ax that they weren't allowed to handle. But he would pretend to hate the job so the teacher would think wood splitting was punishment.

His mind turned to the dog he'd seen lying in the woods. It was a stray dog. It had to be, because Duncan knew every animal within miles of Tideside. It was the biggest, meanest-looking dog he'd ever seen. Usually he paid little attention to animals except to tease them, but there was something about this dog that kept the image of him sharp in Duncan's mind all afternoon. He was big, rough, ugly. Like me, Duncan thought.

Friends

Duncan had been chopping wood for half an hour behind the schoolhouse, and his arms were just now beginning to tire. He loved his own power, and the grudging admiration that his audience was beginning to show. Most of the children had long since gone home, but a few had stayed to watch his punishment.

From inside the school came the voices of the teacher and Amy Walsh, who was practicing for the all-county spelling bee.

"Confident," the teacher barked.

And Amy's voice replied, "Confident — c-o-n, con; f-i, fi; d-e-n-t, dent — confident."

"Good. Now try 'apparent.'"

Duncan thought as he swung the ax, When Amy stays after school, it's just to practice something. It's never for punishment.

But the logical side of his mind answered, Yes, but Amy'd never do something like taking Geordie's lunch away from him.

He couldn't argue with that, so he grew angry and swung harder at the length of oak he was trying to split. His swing was strong, but it had less control than usual, and the ax fell to the side of where he'd wanted to hit. The wood jumped off the chopping stump.

Those watching him began to giggle. Duncan turned toward them, waving the ax in a threatening way, but they backed away only a few steps, toward the safety of the building, and called, "Fatty, fatty, Duncan the fatty."

The chant was unfair. Duncan was large but not really fat. Still, the words hurt him, just as they always did. He felt like a great clumsy ox surrounded by yapping terriers.

Suddenly a movement caught his eye. The gray dog was coming out of the woods toward Duncan. His head was low, his tail wagging very slowly, as though he wasn't sure whether to wag or not.

One little girl gave a tiny shriek, half fun and half fear, and ran for the school steps. The others followed. There was much shrieking and shoving to get up the steps, but their fear was mostly the enjoyable kind, the kind they felt during the telling of ghost stories, when they knew there was little real danger.

"Are you afraid of that old dog?" Duncan called over his shoulder. His voice was thick with scorn.

The Tartar stopped a few yards away from Duncan. Again their eyes met, as they had earlier at the edge of the woods. Duncan was aware of the size and power of the dog, and of the teeth that showed so plainly between the dog's black lips. But he was also aware of the younger children watching him. Duncan's only fame, within the school, lay in his fearlessness and meanness, and that reputation was the most valuable thing he had. Fearlessness and meanness were just about all there was to Duncan Burn, and he had a scary feeling that if he were no longer famous for his courage, he would be nothing at all. Just a big, fat, clumsy nothing.

The huge, sharp-toothed dog was in front of him, possibly mad with rabies. Possibly a wild dog, part wolf. Possibly a killer.

Behind Duncan were the children, waiting,

watching silently, hoping he would give them another chance to make fun of him.

He tossed the ax down behind him and went toward the dog. From deep inside the animal came a low sound that might have been a growl. Duncan had no way of knowing that this was The Tartar's way of expressing joy, or that the dog's trembling was caused by his delight at Duncan's approach.

Duncan went up close to the dog's head, close enough to be bitten if that was what the dog had in mind. Keeping his gaze fastened to the dog's so that he could jump back at the first sign of attack, Duncan reached out and rubbed his knuckles across the animal's skull.

The Tartar's tail began to move. It lashed faster and faster. Suddenly he stood up on his hind legs, braced his front feet on the boy's shoulders, and began licking his face.

For an instant terror froze Duncan. Then the whipping tail and the warm searching tongue made their meaning clear. A thick bubble of warmth rose inside Duncan, a feeling he hadn't had since he was a very small child. It made his eyes sting. It made his arms feel heavy with wanting to wrap themselves around the dog.

But he heard high teasing voices behind him. "Hey, Duncan, that dog's just a big old puppy. He's nothing to be scared of."

"Duncan, get on him and ride him!"

"Go on, Duncan."

Duncan threw one leg over The Tartar's back and pretended to sit on him, although his toes were on the ground. The Tartar began moving gleefully, trying to turn in tight circles to lick the boy's face. For a few moments they romped in a mock show of riding a wild horse. Then Duncan's foot slipped, and the boy and the dog rolled together on the ground.

As the boy fell, The Tartar stared, frightened. He was seeing a small girl in a blue cloak who fell when he played with her and who didn't move again. He was hearing the fear-scream of a girl in a city alleyway as his mouth closed around her arm. He lunged to his feet and stood tense, waiting for the terrible, abrupt end to this new love.

But the boy got up laughing. He shoved The Tartar, and the dog came back against him with shining eyes. Duncan shoved again, but the shove was half a clumsy hug. The joy in The Tartar was coming full strength.

From the school steps came Geordie's voice.

"Duncan, are you going to tie a dead rat to his tail, like you did Mrs. McTier's dog?"

Duncan looked from his audience to the big gray dog who stood waiting for another bout of shoving and lunging. Teasing that little dog of Mrs. McTier's had been fun, tying the dead rat to its tail and watching it go yelping for home, then ducking out of sight before Mrs. McTier could come to the door and see who had done it. The other children had been watching then too, not quite daring to do what Duncan was doing. He had felt like a hero for a few minutes that day.

But now, when he thought of doing something like that to this big gray brute, it didn't seem so smart. He realized that he wouldn't like to humiliate this dog. There was a bond between Duncan and the dog, a bond that was very new but strong and good. It would be like making fun of himself, to make fun of the big gray dog.

But on the other hand, there was his audience. They expected him to do something mean to the dog. After all, he was Duncan Burn. If they knew about the soft warm feeling he had when the dog licked him, they'd call him sissy, laugh at him.

"I don't have a dead rat right now, or else I would," he said.

"Here. Use this." Geordie bounced down from the steps and picked up a branch from a pile of limbs to be broken into kindling. The branch was as long as Geordie was high, and it was fat with leaves and smaller branches. It would rattle enough to frighten any dog if it were tied to his tail. Geordie dragged it triumphantly across the grass to Duncan, but he was very careful not to get too close to the dog. He dropped the branch and bolted back to the steps.

Duncan looked at the branch, then at the dog whose eyes shone with love and trust and eagerness for another game.

"I've got no string," Duncan said flatly, and kicked the branch away.

But Geordie was there, pulling a wad of kite string out of his trousers' pocket.

The ring of small faces watched eagerly from the steps.

Duncan hesitated as long as he could, but he could think of no good reason not to tie the branch onto the dog's tail. At least, no reason the others would believe. With a sinking heart he wondered how long it would take for the love and trust to fade from the dog's eyes.

With fingers that were clumsier than usual, he

knotted one end of the string around the branch.

"Come here, dog."

The Tartar came, wagging and smiling and showing his bottom teeth. Without looking at the dog's eager eyes, Duncan bent and tied the string around the dog's tail. But he tied it loosely, hoping it would slip off before the animal became too frightened.

He stood back. The dog moved to follow him, then felt the pull of the weight on his tail. He ran a few steps but the thing followed, rattling its leaves and poking at his back legs with its twigs. He tried running in tight circles but he couldn't catch it. He sat down and bit at it but it evaded his teeth. Finally he got up, looked at Duncan, and moved across the grass to his new friend. He stopped in front of Duncan, then swung around so that the boy would see what was bothering him and fix it.

Duncan watched and understood. Suddenly he didn't care what the others thought of him. This dog was more important to him than all the kids in the world. This dog trusted him, looked up to him, came to him for help even though it was Duncan himself who had caused the hurt.

He untied the string and ran his hand roughly

over the place on the dog's tail where the string had been, trying to erase the feel of it, the memory of it, in the same way he erased the chalk from the blackboard.

The Tartar turned and jumped up against the boy, delighted that the thing was gone from his tail.

Duncan took the branch and threw it as far as he could. Then he turned to the children on the steps and made an announcement.

"From now on, this is my dog, and anybody that does anything mean to him, I'm going to beat up so hard they'll bleed for a week."

"You're mine, old dog!"

"I've got a dog."

Duncan made the announcement from the cottage door. His voice sounded as though he were already arguing, although no one had yet told him he couldn't keep the dog.

His mother was putting the supper on to boil. The cottage was only one room with a sleeping loft, and just then the room seemed completely filled with children. Over the heads between them, Mrs. Burn stared at Duncan and The Tartar.

"Where did that beast come from? Wherever it was, take him back to it." She turned back to her pots.

"He didn't come from anywhere. He was at the school. He's my dog, and if he can't stay, I won't stay either."

"Tittle-tattle. You're not but ten — "

"I'm twleve, Mother. It's Tommy that's ten."

"Twelve then. Still too young to be talking about leaving home. And too old to sass your mother. You'll not be keeping any rigwoody old dog in here, not when we don't have the room nor the food for all you young ones."

Duncan had expected that. He had thought about it while he finished the wood splitting and while he walked home with the dog cantering in circles around him. He knew what to say to her, but he was still afraid of what the final answer would be. The only thing he was sure of was that this dog was the most important thing that had ever happened to him and that, if necessary, he would leave home to be with the dog.

"Mother, he's got to be my dog. That's all there is to it. I'll make a place for him to sleep outside, and I'll figure out some way to feed him."

His mother turned to look at him again, and her eyes held a warning. Duncan's words were dangerously close to sassy. But before she could say anthing more, a shrill quarrel broke out between two of the children at her feet.

"Here now! Rob. Willie, er — Eddie, I mean. Give over and hush yourselves. Duncan, I'm too busy to argue with you about the beast. If he's here, he's here, but he'll not set foot inside my house, and I'll not give him a bite to eat."

Duncan turned and ran to the rock seawall down the hill from the cottage, and The Tartar galloped beside him.

"You're mine, old dog! I don't know yet how I'll get the money to feed you, but I'll do it someway."

Duncan slowed to a walk. The dog has been a stray, he thought. He's been getting his own food from somewhere, so I suppose he could go on getting it for himself, at least for a while.

But a strong new urge was waking inside Duncan, the urge to take care of this dog, to provide what he needed, to be his master in every sense. Never before had Duncan felt this way about anything; never before had anything, or anyone, depended on him. Duncan pulled the dog's head close.

He walked along the broad top of the seawall, jumping from stone to stone, with The Tartar leaping along the landward side of the wall. When they were well away from the village, Duncan sat down on the wall. The Tartar leaped up beside him and sat, breathing his hot breath into the boy's face.

He can sleep in the woodshed, Duncan thought. I'll make him a bed out of seaweed, and it'll be as soft and warm as my own bed. Later on, when I get old enough to leave home and be on my own, he and I will have a cottage all of our own somewhere, and he'll sleep on my bed with me. I'll think of some way to buy food for him.

Let's see, what could I do? Work after school and earn money? No, there's nobody in Tideside who would hire me. There's already more people who want to work than there is work to go around. Except in summer, when the day-trippers and holiday people come.

He thought about the holiday crowds that came to the inns at Tideside in the summer. They spent money, lots of it. But what did he have to offer that nobody else had?

After a few minutes of pondering, the answer came. "A very big strong dog," he thought out loud. "All right now, go from there. What can a big strong dog do?"

In spite of the seriousness of the problem, Duncan found himself enjoying the challenge of trying to solve it. Until now, most of the problems he had had to put his mind to were silly school problems, mathematics or themes to be written. Things that didn't matter to him. Now he had to use his mind, really use it, and he was surprised to find that it worked. It occurred to him that there might be more to Duncan Burn than toughness, after all.

Then his thoughts returned to his problems. What can a big dog do? Pull something, like a wagon or a cart. Or— But he could think of nothing else that a large dog would be good at. So he went back to thinking about a cart.

I could probably make a harness for him, and if those bicycle wheels are still in the junk pile behind the store, that would be a start. But what would be the point? A pony could haul a much heavier load than he could, so who would want to hire him? And besides, it would be mean to try to make a draft horse out of him. He's a dog. My dog.

For an instant he remembered the way the dog had looked at him as he was tying the branch to his tail.

"Duncan," a child's voice called to him. He

turned to see one of his small brothers running down the grassy slope toward him.

"That's a nice doggie," Rob chanted as he reached to slap his dirty little hand against The Tartar's ribs. The Tartar moved happily under Duncan's arm.

"You better watch out, Rob. He's mean, and if I tell him to he'll bite you."

Rob backed off a step, studied The Tartar, then decided Duncan was just teasing him again.

"Can I ride on him?" Rob piped.

"Don't be daft. He's a dog, not a pony. You don't ride on dogs."

Suddenly Duncan remembered something he'd seen last fall at the Wigtown Sheep Dog Trials. Behind the area of refreshment booths and coconut-bowling booths, a man had been selling dog-cart rides to a long line of children. The dog was a mastiff, huge and heavy and bred for such work, but Duncan's dog was just as big.

The picture filled Duncan's imagination — he and the dog and a brightly painted cart, giving rides along the beach while the holiday people waited in lines to hand him their shillings. Maybe he'd even be ready for next month's sheep dog trials.

"Duncan!" Rob's voice rose to a shrill demand.

"What, you pesty little midge-fly?"

"You didn't answer me."

"What did you say?"

With all the patience of a four-year-old, Rob repeated, "I said, what's the doggie's name?"

"I haven't decided yet," Duncan said haughtily. "I'm not going to give him just any old name. It has to be perfect."

Yes, he thought, for a dog like this he would have to think of exactly the right name. But he couldn't be bothered with that now. He had work to do. Plans to make.

He jumped down from the seawall. "Come on, dog. Let's go find those wheels. Go on home, Rob. I don't want you in the way."

Dog Cart

It was noon of the next day, and Duncan sat with his back against a tree trunk at the edge of the school yard. The Tartar lay beside him, having spent the morning in the woods near the school, hunting rabbits.

Duncan's oatcake disappeared without ever having been tasted. The boy's mind was filled with problems of wheels, harness, seats, and how to hold them all together. He hardly noticed when Geordie began edging toward him.

"Are you going to keep the dog, Duncan?" the little boy asked cautiously.

"Yes. And I've trained him to attack anyone I tell him to, and bite them. So you'd better not come too close."

The expression on Geordie's face was mixed. He was pretty sure Duncan was teasing him, but on the other hand, it was an awfully big dog. And mean looking. When Geordie looked from The Tartar to Duncan, and saw the closeness between the two of them, a new kind of respect came into his eyes. Duncan had very obviously conquered an animal that the rest of them were afraid of, and to Geordie that was proof that Duncan really was as fearless as he had always said he was. Geordie felt the beginning of something like hero worship.

"Duncan."

"What?"

"I'm eating bread and cheese."

"I see you are. Shut up and go away. I'm busy."

"What are you busy doing? You look like you're just sitting there."

Duncan brought his mind away from dog carts and focused on Geordie. He thought he could see a glimmer of respect in the little boy's eyes. Suddenly Geordie didn't seem like such a bad little midge. Playing to the respect that Geordie might be starting to show him, Duncan said, "I'm making plans. I'm going to fix up a cart for my dog. It's going to be red, with silver wheels, and nobody can ride in it unless I say so."

Geordie's eyes became round and dark with wonder. He stared from Duncan to the gray giant lying beside him.

"Does he know how to pull a cart?" Geordie whispered, his voice filled with awe.

Duncan said, haughtily, "He'll do whatever I tell him to."

"Oh." Geordie settled back in a squat on his heels and silently ate his lunch, staring from Duncan to The Tartar.

By the end of the week everyone in Tideside, at least everyone who was not blind and deaf, knew about Duncan Burn's new dog and the cart that was being assembled for selling rides to children at the sheep dog trials and on the beach next summer. Men, working in teams to fold the fishnets into the boats, said, "Did ye see that great brute of a dog Duncan's got? I'd not like to have him angry with me."

"They say the boy's going to sell dog-cart rides. P'raps the lad has got a head on him, for making a penny. I'd not thought he had anything in him but devilment."

And the women, pausing at one another's door-sills, said, "I misdoubt that young Duncan can manage the beast. I seen the two of 'em jumping and tearing around on the brae like they was both daft. I'd never let a child of mine ride with 'em."

"Aye, that's true, Mary, but I'll tell you one thing. My Geordie doesn't come home from school now crying because Duncan was bullying him. If a dog will do that for the lad, then I say it's a blessing he's got one."

It was Saturday afternoon, and the cart was nearly done. Duncan and The Tartar stood inside the blacksmith shop, watching while Duncan's Uncle Tommy joined two battered bicycle wheels to an axle rod that had been lying around the shop for years. In the doorway lay a small wicker seat from a pony cart. Duncan had found the seat, and a pair of pony shafts, behind the stable of an abandoned country estate near Tideside.

Duncan said, "Be sure to make it so the wheels

will turn easy, Uncle Tommy. I don't want the dog to work any harder than he has to."

"Aye, lad. I know. But you've nothing to worry about. The cart won't weigh but a wee bit, and these wheels'll go like silk, once we get them on and oiled. What are you going to use for harness?"

"I don't know yet," Duncan answered, stooping to rough the dog's ears. "I was thinking about a bit of rope, but I don't want to rub sores on him, and besides, I'd like something prettier."

Uncle Tommy turned to stare thoughtfully at the dog. "You'd not want pony harness. It would be too big and too heavy. We'll have to think on it a bit."

Aunt Martha, who had been listening and watching from the door that led into the house, turned and disappeared.

"She's got a drop of juice for us, I think," Uncle Tommy said. He went back to work, and to the song he'd been singing under his breath. " 'And here's a hand, my trusty fere, and give us a hand of thine; and we'll take a right good willie-waught for auld lang syne.' "

"A bit early in the season for 'Auld Lang Syne,' isn't it?" Duncan teased. He was happy this afternoon, happier than he could ever remember being before. The cart was taking shape, people were being nice to him — in his happiness he sang a bit of Uncle Tommy's song aloud.

"What's a 'fere,' Uncle Tommy?" he asked, interrupting his own tune.

"A fere? Why, it's," Uncle Tommy paused to think, "it's a companion. A trusted companion."

"Oh." Duncan looked down at the dog. "My trusty fere," he whispered.

When Aunt Martha appeared, it was not drinks she was carrying; it was an armload of long silver strips. Duncan stared at them, felt them with his fingers. They were about an inch wide, yards and yards long, and silvery white with a single red thread down the middle. They were some sort of finely woven material; Duncan had never seen anything like it before.

"It's parachute cording," the woman explained. "My sister that works in the parachute factory in London gets these pieces free. They're leftovers, or something, and last time she was up, she brought me a huge bag of them. I've no use for them, so if you want them for your harness, take them along. They're nylon, as strong as anything you could want."

Duncan took the armload and stammered his thanks. It was perfect. Light, strong, flat and smooth and comfortable for the dog, and pretty besides.

"Now we've got it all," he sang silently. The Tartar caught his mood and began racing wildly about the cluttered shop.

Suddenly the happiness in Duncan was replaced by worry. I've been so busy thinking about the cart, he thought, I never stopped to worry about whether I can get him to settle down and pull it. If he goes to acting wild and crazy like that, with a wee child in the cart, it'll be terrible trouble.

An Understanding

The cart and harness were done. The wicker basket seat was firmly bolted to the axle between the wheels, and the wheels were bolted to the shafts. Uncle Tommy had donated a bit of red paint he'd had left over from painting his barn, and enough silver paint to cover the wheels. The effect of the red cart with its shining silver wheels was so beautiful that Duncan could hardly look away from it.

The cart stood just outside the Burn cottage, glistening in the sun. In the grass beside it lay the harness. Duncan had intended to put it together simply by tying knots in it, but his mother had come bustling and grumbling out of the cottage with the stout cord she used to sew the edging onto his father's fishnets. She did a great deal of scolding about foolishness and great ugly beasts, but while she grumbled she was holding lengths of silver cording up to The Tartar, cutting, stitching, and fitting again.

Duncan was so happy that he didn't know how to hold the happiness in. As soon as his mother was finished using the dog for fittings, Duncan fell on him with a wild rush. It was the only way his happiness could come out without exploding. And the dog seemed to feel the same way. They rolled on the ground; they got up and raced to the seawall and back, leaping, shouting, barking. "Acting the fool," Mrs. Burn muttered around tight-pressed lips that held her thread.

It was Sunday afternoon, and as word spread through Tideside that Duncan was almost ready to try the dog in the cart, children and a few grown-ups began strolling toward the Burn cottage to watch.

When the last stitch was in place and his mother had grumbled her way back into the cottage, Duncan called the dog.

"All right now, settle down. This is serious. You've got to stand still and learn to pull the cart. Stop it," he said sharply as the dog leaped against him. "No playing now. This is work. We have to earn that money so I can feed you. And we have to show them." He glanced at his growing audience. "Do you understand?"

At this new soft pleading tone in the boy's voice, The Tartar quit jumping and stood to listen, his head cocked.

Duncan led him to the harness, gave him a few minutes to sniff it, then began sliping it on over his head. The Tartar stood stiff and wary.

"He ain't going to like it," a man said.

Duncan tried to ignore the remark, and the others that followed.

The Tartar was not fightened by the harness, at least not after the first strange moments of feeling it around his chest and ribs. Mrs. Burn had also made a long lead strap with a collar loop in one end. Duncan slipped the loop over the dog's head, carefully folded the trailing traces across the dog's back, and tried to lead him.

The Tartar braced his huge feet at the pull of the collar. Someone else had tied a rope around his neck once, someone he had trusted, and the rope had held him to a tree in the middle of a frightening darkness while the man disappeared from his life.

But Duncan said softly, "It's all right, lad. I'll not hurt you. Come along now."

The Tartar relaxed and allowed himself to be led around the cottage once, twice. It began to be fun, walking connected to the boy.

Duncan brought him to a stop beside the cart and let him take a long, slow, sniffing look at it. Then he called, still holding his voice to a soft note, "Rob, Geordie, come give us a hand now. I'll stand here and hold him so he won't run off, and each of you get on one side of the cart. Easy now, don't go rushing up to him. That's better. Now take the shafts and bring them up here so I can fasten the traces."

The Tartar rolled his eyes in an effort to see what was going on behind him, but as long as Duncan's fingers were scratching him under the neck, he was willing to stand.

The shafts were in place on either side of the dog, and Duncan snapped the traces. The cart was hitched.

Once again Duncan led the dog around the cottage, and this time a shiny, squeaky contraption followed so closely behind The Tartar that he could feel it against his tail. He remembered the branch that had gotten itself attached to his tail a few days ago. He remembered that the boy had taken it off of him. He stopped and looked pleadingly up at the boy, wanting him to get this new annoyance off of his tail.

But Duncan said, "Come along now, lad. You'll have to get used to it. It won't hurt you."

After several jostling, jarring attempts at bolting away from the cart, the dog settled down and allowed himself to be convinced by the boy's voice. He realized the cart wasn't hurting him and it was so light he could hardly feel the drag o it against his chest.

Finally Duncan said, "I think he's ready to tr it with a passenger. Rob, get in."

The little boy gave a squeal of excitement and ran to the basket seat. Clumsily he scrambled up into it, clutching at the iron handholds on either side as it rocked beneath him. But before he could get turned around to sit down, The Tartar leaped, the cart tipped, and Rob was spilled to the ground.

Duncan crooned, "Easy, lad. You *have* to stand still."

The Tartar's tail thrashed. Excitement was rising in him. He was the center of attention, the center of some sort of game. All of his instincts told him to break free and run with Duncan across the grass, to roll and leap and bark with the joy of it.

Rob picked himself up off the ground. When he bent to brush the grass from his legs, he saw a few drops of blood coming to the surface of his scraped knees. Immediately his face drew into a pucker and he ran, crying, into the cottage.

Duncan sighed. "Now see what you've done, with your jumping about. Willie, you're next. Hop up."

But Willie shook his head in reluctant defiance of his older brother. "He might hurt me, Duncan. I don't want to."

Duncan gave him a look of concentrated disgust. "All right, sissy. Eddie, how about you?"

Eddie said nothing, but moved a step closer to the cottage door.

Suddenly Geordie came forward. "I'll help you, Duncan," he said in a small voice.

Duncan looked down at him. "You're not scared?"

Geordie stared down at his toes. "I'm a wee bit scared of you," he admitted, "but not of the dog."

Duncan felt a flush of shame, but it lasted only a moment. That other Duncan who used to pick on Geordie seemed to be someone else entirely. That was the old mean Duncan. This one had more important business to concern himself with. He was the owner of the biggest, best dog in Tideside, not to mention a red-and-silver dogcart.

He turned his attention back to the dog. "Now you've got to hold still. *Please*. It's important. All right, Geordie, hop up."

Duncan tightened his hold on the dog's collar. When The Tartar felt the teetering of the cart shafts, he moved to try to turn around and play with the boys.

"Be still." Duncan's voice was pleading now.

The Tartar paused, tilted his head, and looked up at Duncan. And slowly he began to understand. The boy didn't want him to play no This was serious. This was work. Somewhere in the back of his memory came the picture of a man and a collie working soberly together, of the man's hand on the dog's head, and of his own longing to know that kind of closeness with a master.

He stood quietly.

Geordie settled himself in the seat, his hands clenched hard around the handholds on the arms, his fat legs sticking straight out.

Cautiously Duncan said, "Away we go, lad."

Dog, cart, rider, and leader moved slowly, smoothly, around the cottage yard.

After Geordie had clambered into and out of the cart several times, and the dog had pulled him on countless rounds of the yard, Duncan was at last sure that the dog was to be trusted with wee children in the cart. He told Geordie he could run on home now, and he thanked bi his help.

Geordie smiled, turned to go, th ᴀ esi-tantly back. He looked down and said swiftly, "I'm not scared of you anymore, either, Duncan." Then he turned and ran.

Duncan stood watching him go. For the first time in years he felt completely good. For the first time in years he liked himself. He sat down and took the dog's long ugly head between his hands.

"My Fere."

They stood quietly for a moment; then Duncan began unsnapping the harness.

"Come on, Fere. Let's get you out of that. You've worked enough for one day. I'll race you to the seawall."

His answer was the dog's low growl of happiness.

About the Author

Ms. Hall was born in a suburb of Chicago and was raised in Des Moines, Iowa. She has always loved dogs and horses and has kept them around her whenever possible. As a child, she was limited to stray dogs, neighbors' horses, and the animals found in library books. But as an adult she has owned and shown several horses and has worked with dogs, both as a veterinarian's assistant and a handler on the dog show circuit. Many of her books are about dogs and horses.

Ms. Hall lives in a one-hundred-year-old farmhouse near the village of Garnavillo, Iowa. Besides writing, she works as coordinator and counselor for a local telephone counseling service offering help to troubled young people. Her leisure time is spent reading, playing the piano, or exploring the nearby hills and woodlands on horseback or foot, with a dog or two at her heels.